Going to the doctor

Anne Civardi

Edited by Michelle Bates

Illustrated by Stephen Cartwright

Cover design by Jan McCafferty

Medical adviser: Catherine Sims BSc; MBBS and Dr.Lance King

There is a little yellow duck hiding on every page. Can you find it?

This is the Jay family.

Jenny has woken up with a bad cough and Jack has hurt his arm.
They must go and see the doctor.

Mrs. Jay phones the doctor.

She makes an appointment while Mr. Jay helps Jack get dressed.
"Ow," shouts Jack, "watch my arm, Dad."

The Jays go to see the doctor.

Mrs. Jay takes Jack, Jenny and Joey to see Doctor Woody. "We've got an appointment at 2 o'clock," she tells the receptionist.

The receptionist checks her book.

"Yes, it's for Jack and Jenny, isn't it?" she says. "And for Joey too," Mrs. Jay reminds her. "He needs to have his immunization."

The Jays sit in the waiting room.

There are lots of people waiting to see the doctor. Mrs. Jay reads
a book to Jenny. Jack and Joey want to play.

Now it is the Jays' turn.

Doctor Woody calls their name. "Who shall I see first?" she says.
"Me," says Jack, holding out his arm.

Doctor Woody examines Jack.

She looks at his sore arm. "It's not broken," she says, "but you do have a sprained wrist, Jack."

Doctor Woody puts Jack's arm in a sling.

"Just wear this for a few days," Doctor Woody tells him. "It will feel better soon."

Doctor Woody checks Jenny.

She takes her temperature with a thermometer. Then she looks down Jenny's throat. "It's very red," she says.

Then she examines Jenny's ears with an auroscope. "Your ears are fine," she tells Jenny.

Doctor Woody listens to Jenny's breathing with a stethoscope. "Breathe in and out deeply," she says.

She feels Jenny's neck to see if her glands are swollen. "You have a slight chest infection," she says.

Jenny needs some medicine.

Doctor Woody prints a prescription for Jenny from her computer. Then she sits down at her desk and signs it.

Now it is Joey's turn.

Doctor Woody gives Joey his immunization. It only hurts a little.

She also gives Joey some drops so that he won't get polio. Then she says goodbye to the Jays.

The Jays pick up Jenny's prescription.

Mrs. Jay stops at the pharmacy. She gives the pharmacist the prescription and he gives her some medicine.

At home, Mrs. Jay puts Jenny to bed.

Mrs. Jay tucks Jenny in and gives her a spoonful of medicine.
"You'll be better soon," she says.

That evening, Mr. Jay comes home from work.

"Hello everyone," he says. "How are you all?" Jack jumps to his feet.
"Joey's all right, and Jenny's in bed," he says. "But look at my sling!"

First published in 1992. This revised edition published in 2000 by Usborne Publishing Ltd, Usborne House, 83-85 Saffron Hill, London EC1N 8RT, England
Copyright © 2000, 1992 Usborne Publishing Ltd.
First published in America in 2001
The name Usborne and the device ⊕ are Trade Marks of Usborne Publishing Ltd.